Murder at Sophie's Salon

A Jessica Gray Cozy Mystery

Jane T. O'Brien

This book is fiction. All characters, events, and organizations portrayed in this novel are the product of the author's imagination or used fictitiously. Any resemblance to actual persons - living or dead - is entirely coincidental.

ISBN: 9798836774059
Imprint: Independently published

Mystery Series by Jane T. O'Brien

Samantha Degan Cozy Mystery Series

Murder in Stonehill Manor
Murder in Lancashire
Murder in Ashville
Murder at Seabrook Shores
(Includes Murder in Pepperberry Lake a short story)

Molly Ryan Cozy Mystery Series

Murder in Hillsboro
Murder in Kincaid Towers
Murder in Evergreen
Murder at Coventry Hill Inn

Cassandra Cross Cozy Mystery Series

Murder on the Isabella
Murder at Channel Two
Murder in Newcastle
Murder at Cranberry Creek

Rebecca Snow Cozy Mystery Series

Murder in Oakwood Park
Murder on Bradbury Hill
Murder on Applewood Circle
Murder at Lake Willoughby

Avery Fox Cozy Mystery Series

Murder in Somerset County
Murder in Hidden Oaks
Murder on Ravenwood Campus
Murder in Clearview Park

Katie McDougal Cozy Mystery Series

Murder in Brookhaven
Murder in Rosedale Hospital
Murder at Driftwood Bay
Murder at Fall River Resort

Sarah Delaney Cozy Mystery Series

Murder in Woodbridge
Murder on Cottonwood Bluff
Murder in Eagle Crest Manor
Murder on Danforth Island

Jessica Gray Cozy Mystery Series

Murder in Brentwood
Murder in Chelsea Gardens
Murder at Cromwell, Inc.
Murder at Sophie's Salon

Other Books by Jane T. O'Brien

Novels

Bristol Falls
Glenwood Hills
Cumberland Heights

Cozy Mysteries

Murder in Forest Glen
The Mystery of Shelby Lake
The Mystery of Waverly Island
Murder in Pinewood Bluff

Life in Camden Corners
A Continuing Saga
Parts One through Twelve

Children's Books

Finian Frog Series

Fabulous Finian Frog
Finian Frog Falls in Love
Finian Frog and Farley's Wishes
Finian Frog and Froglet Freddy

Hennessey Hound Tales Series

Happy Hennessey Hound
Hennessey Hound and the Bully

The author of Murder at Sophie's Salon has no formal writing training and simply enjoys telling stories.

The writing style is not for everyone. You will be sorely disappointed if you expect the great American novel.

I am grateful to everyone who reads and supports my efforts.

The Characters

Jessica Gray is an aspiring mystery writer with an affinity for resolving mysteries in her own backyard. To help pay the bills, the law school graduate works in her father's law firm. Jessica's curiosity often puts her in the middle of dangerous situations.

Richard (Rick) Madison, a detective on the Brentwood Police Force, is Jessica's childhood friend. Rick is also a mystery writer and has had success with two publications. After a twenty-year separation, the friends reunite and find love.

Meredith Donovan, an attorney in the Steven Gray law practice. Meredith is married to Jack Donovan. Together, they are parents to Jack's precocious daughter, Lucy.

Travis Bloom is the son of notorious gangster, Harry Bloom and his socialite wife, Sylvia. Travis strives to bring honor to the Bloom name by living an exemplary life. He meets and falls in love with hairstylist, Sophie Clark.

Prologue

The annual New Year's Eve gala at the Brentwood Country Club is held tonight. The public is invited to attend the party, joining their friends and neighbors to celebrate the coming year in style.

The finest hair salon in Brentwood, Casa di Giorgio, is bustling with partygoers searching for a glamorous new hairstyle for the event.

In his signature shiny plum-colored shirt, Giorgio visits each station to fawn over his customers as their hair is styled by his talented staff. He meticulously tweaks a curl or fiddles with a wave, even though fine-tuning is unnecessary.

Fresh out of beauty school, Sophie Clark was thrilled to be hired as a stylist at Casa di Giorgio. Sophie's dream was to purchase a shop with her inheritance from her grandfather. Fearing Giorgio's wrath, she put aside her dream.

On the day of the gala, while the busy stylists worked their magic, Giorgio glided through the shop, smiling and accepting praise from delighted patrons.

Since opening the salon, Giorgio had never been seen picking up a shampoo bottle or plugging in a hair dryer.

Chapter One

As he approached his thirty-seventh birthday, Hank Henshaw woke one morning resolving to reinvent himself. Instead of going to his job on a construction site, he enrolled in the local beauty college in his hometown.

After receiving his beautician license, he traveled to New York City. His charm and charisma helped him land a job at an exclusive salon with an affluent clientele. His time was spent shampooing hair and schmoozing with customers. He watched and learned the ins and outs of running a successful upscale salon.

Taking a cue from the single-named likes of Bono and Prince, Hank Henshaw transformed himself into Giorgio. Only his banker and the IRS knew his given name. A sophisticated look was established with a new haircut and a well-groomed beard adorning his handsome face.

Knowing he could not make his mark competing in New York, Giorgio chose to open a salon in Brentwood. He hired stylists from the local beauty school. After weeding out the mediocre and keeping the best, he opened Casa Di Giorgio. The elegant salon was unlike anything the town had seen. The stylists all looked like models with trendy uniforms and perfectly styled hair. Many women had secret crushes on the proprietor, others not so secret.

Sophie Clark was one of those selected to work at the salon. As a stylist, she had a charming personality and knew how to achieve the look her clients desired.

* * *

When Casa Di Giorgio opened its doors more than five years ago, curiosity got the better of Jessica Gray. She had heard her friends talking about the upscale hair salon and the dreamy owner with only one name. When she called to make an appointment with Giorgio, she was instead scheduled with Sophie.

Jessica did not complain; she liked the way Sophie styled her hair. Through the years, Jessica has referred her family and many friends to Sophie for their hair care.

Jessica noticed Giorgio spent more time in his office than in the salon with customers. She asked if the man was even a hairdresser.

Sophie laughed, saying she saw his license on the wall of his office, but she had never seen him do more than interfere with the other's work. Giorgio pretends to be this high-class stylist from New York City. He does not fool me."

Jessica could tell that Sophie did not care for her boss by the look on her face.

"Sophie, you are so talented. Have you thought about going out on your own?"

"Do not let Giorgio hear you say that. He will throw us both out. I would like nothing better than to start my own salon."

"What is standing in your way, Sophie?"

"Giorgio hired me right out of beauty school. I wanted to work in his salon to gain experience. I had to agree to his terms and sign a five-year contract before he would hire me. Others did the same, and now we are stuck."

"Meredith Donovan is an attorney. She is a client of yours. I know because I recommended you to her. She can get you out of the contract."

"Giorgio threatened to blackball me if I did not fulfill my contract. He would do it and make sure I cannot bring my customers along with me."

"I did not sign a contract with him, and he cannot keep me here. I will follow you wherever you go, and my friends will too."

Sophie was determined to wait out the contract. She tried not to make waves with Giorgio. The man was a bully who cheated his staff out of their tip money by taking a generous portion for himself. They purchased supplies from a company that compensated Giorgio for his loyalty.

* * *

Sophie's contract was scheduled to expire at midnight. With the New Year's Eve gala tonight, she had double the reason to celebrate.

Jessica sat in the chair at Sophie's station." Today is your last day under the thumb of Giorgio. I am so happy for you."

"Meredith was in earlier. Everything is going on schedule. Soon, I will be the new owner of a vacant shop." Sophie laughed nervously.

"Does Giorgio suspect you are leaving his control?"

"He mentioned signing another contract next week. I did not let on that I had no interest in his contract or him. Now, let us get you glammed up for the big night. Mindy and I are going together. Who knows, we might each find someone special tonight? Not that I will have time to think about dating for a while."

Mindy Lawrence and other stylists plan to leave Giorgio in favor of Sophie's new place. Jessica had a sinking feeling Giorgio would not be pleased.

Chapter Two

Jessica returned home from the Salon. She laid her new gown on her bed. She laughed, remembering the day last week shopping for the perfect dress for the New Year's Eve Gala. The two grandmothers, Betty Gray and Rebecca Sloan, were like teenagers choosing their prom dresses. Jessica, her mother, Karen, and twin sister, Natalie, giggled as the older women tried on several dresses before finding their favorites.

Since the day after Christmas, Brentwood's dress shops and department stores have been flooded with customers. The city has been buzzing with anticipation ahead of the gala.

Jessica holds up her dress, hoping it is not too revealing. Natalie had talked her into allowing a scant amount of cleavage to show. "You have a great figure, so why not show it off?"

* * *

After two kids, Natalie looks like she did in high school. Last month, a salesperson mistook her for a teenaged babysitter. It made her happy until she remembered her hair had been in pigtails. She is busy with the children and her volunteer work but vows to fix her hair before leaving the house.

When her husband, Ken, sees her, he gives a wolf whistle that causes the dog to run and hide under the bed.

"Mommy, you are a princess," exclaims Leah. Ryan's eyes light up. He likes the sparkles on his mother's fancy dress.

* * *

Detective Rick Madison arrives at Jessica's apartment. Rick and Jessica were childhood friends when their families spent the summers on Brentwood Shores. After more than twenty years, their paths crossed again. The youthful crushes turned into love. Rick joined the Brentwood Police Force to be near Jessica. The couple, both mystery writers, have been inseparable ever since. Jessica works at her father's law firm and often finds herself in the middle of a real-life mystery.

"Is this monkey suit necessary, Jessie? Whose bright idea was this fancy-schmancy party?"

"Stop complaining. Mom said Dad is balking too. He wants to stay home to watch the ball drop on television. I spent a small fortune on my dress. The least you can do is admire it."

Rick stepped into the room to see his best girl more clearly. His eyes open wide. "You look terrific." He decides a little discomfort is worth having Jessica on his arm.

"I should have brought you a corsage. I feel like I am going to senior prom."

"Where would you pin a corsage on this dress? Natalie talked me into it. I hope it is not too risqué for Brentwood."

"It's perfect, and so are you." Rick took her in his arms. "You did something different with your hair. You look like a movie star."

"I must admit, I feel like one, too. I have not told you how great you look. Let us go dazzle the partygoers."

"Or we could stay home and watch the ball drop. I like your dad's idea."

Jessica gave him a friendly punch on the arm, and they were out the door.

* * *

The elder Grays arrived at the gala with the widowed Rebecca Sloan. Eighty-year-old Dennis walked proudly into the country club with the two women on his arms. The Grays and the Sloan family had been charter members of Brentwood Country Club and were well known to the staff. They were happy the club had opened its doors to non-members for the occasion. Some members were appalled by the decision and refused to attend. Jessica thinks the party will be more fun without the pompous stuffed shirts.

* * *

Sophie Clark and her friend, Mindy, cautiously enter the country club.

"We should not have come, Sophie. We do not belong in a fancy place like this with all the rich people."

"You are the one who talked me into coming. You cannot back out now. Jessica Gray is sitting with her family. She and her sister look so glamorous. We outdid ourselves on their hair today."

Standing at the door, Sophie and Mindy, looking self-conscious, caught Jessica's attention. She calls
from the table, inviting them to join their party.

"We do not want to intrude on your family gathering."

After repeated coaxing, the newcomers join the group.

Travis Bloom stopped by the table to say hello. His eyes twinkled when Jessica introduced him to Sophie.

"Travis, you are welcome to sit with us."

"I'd like that," he said with his eyes glued to Sophie.

* * *

After dinner, the band played various tunes for both young and old. Travis invited Sophie to dance.

As they danced, Sophie said, "Travis, I am only a hairstylist. I am one of the outsiders invited tonight."

"Are you saying I need a different haircut? I have been going to the same barber for years. It is time for a change."

"Your hair is perfect. I am not soliciting business. You are a lawyer; I cut hair. We live in different circles. I am out of your league."

"What do your parents do for a living, Sophie?"

She looked at him questioningly. "Dad is a salesman; my mom is a dental receptionist."

"My dad is a crook, and my mom is a social butterfly. I would say I am out of your league."

Sophie smiled. She hopes she will be next to Travis Bloom when the clock strikes midnight. She looks forward to her first kiss of the new year.

Chapter Three

As the new year draws closer, anticipation grows in the country club ballroom. Laughter and joy fill the air.

Travis and Sophie step onto the balcony to breathe in the brisk air. He places his jacket on her shoulders. The temptation to kiss her is thwarted when they hear a voice behind them.

"I see they have let any riffraff into the place tonight."

Without turning, Sophie knows it is Giorgio who is standing behind her.

"You must have drawn the short stick to get stuck with this one, Buddy."

As Travis was about to clobber the jerk, Sophie put her hand on his arm.

"What is it with you and the color purple, Giorgio?" He is wearing a purple velvet tuxedo jacket.

"You must admit, I look great tonight. Where did you buy your get-up? Good Will?"

"That is enough, Buddy. Find someone else to harass. The lady and I are enjoying a pleasant evening."

"She's no lady." Giorgio laughed. "Do not forget, you have a contract to sign. That is, if I decide, I want you to continue working for me."

Sophie scowled as he walked away. "Where were we?" She asks, but the spell has been broken.

* * *

Giorgio sashays throughout the crowd, stopping to fawn over the women he has pegged as influential.

Jessica turns to her sister. Giorgio is making nice with Olivia Talbot. Shall we tell him about the last man who made eyes at Reggie Talbot's wife?"

"No, a broken nose on that pretty face will serve him right."

Sophie and Travis return to the table. "I see Giorgio is up to his tricks with Mrs. Talbot. I would not put it past him to kiss the woman at midnight."

As the countdown begins, Giorgio sees the look in Mr. Talbot's eyes and backs off.

Three... Two... One... Happy New Year. The band plays Auld Lang Syne.

With everyone kissing around them, Travis smiles, taking Sophie in his arms as they share a kiss.

With Travis by her side and her contract with Giorgio ended, Sophie's heart is full of hope for the new year.

The party is over for the older folks. Dennis Gray comments that it is four hours past his bedtime. Steve and Karen call it a night, along with the folks who need to relieve their babysitters.

"I did not hear one complaint about your monkey suit, Rick. Did you have an enjoyable time?"

"I must admit, it was a nice party. We should dance more often. Shall we take one more turn around the dance floor before leaving?"

Jessica loves being in Rick's arms whether they are dancing or not.

* * *

Taking a break to catch her breath, Mindy sits at the table alone. She danced with every eligible man at the party.

"Mindy is sitting alone; I should sit with her. She will feel self-conscious by herself."

Travis doubted the girl had a self-conscious bone in her body after he had watched her dance with everyone under the age of sixty-five but did not argue.

"Mindy, how about a nightcap before we call it a night?"

"That sounds good. I am a bit parched from dancing."

When Travis left the table, Mindy smiled at Sophie. "You found yourself a prince tonight; I was stuck with all the frogs."

"Mindy, you looked like you were having the time of your life. I did not see any frogs."

"Those guys are all rich; they would never be interested in a lowly hairstylist. Travis is rich as well, but he is crazy about you. I can tell."

"Travis is not crazy about me; we just met." Sophie hopes her friend's observation is correct.

Travis returns to the table with their drinks. “Mindy, what is the matter? Did one of those bozos do something stupid?”

“No, they were perfect gentlemen.”

“Mindy was on her feet all day and danced the night away. She is exhausted; I had better take her home.”

“I’d ask you for breakfast tomorrow, but considering the hour, how about lunch.”

“I would like that.” Sophie jotted her number on a napkin.

* * *

“I can take care of myself, Travis. There is no need to follow me home.”

“It is New Year's Eve; the roads are clogged with people who have over-celebrated. I will not come in; I want to be sure you arrive home safely. Humor me.”

Sophie felt disappointed when she heard him say he would not come in. She knew it was too early in the relationship for that step, but her heart told her differently.

Chapter Four

Driving home in his leased sports car, Giorgio thought about Olivia Talbot. *She cannot be more than thirty-five. What is a looker like her doing with that old guy?* Giorgio knew the answer. Reggie Talbot is a billionaire.

Giorgio lived frugally to accumulate wealth. After five years, he is on his way. His lease on the building housing Casa Di Giorgio includes a private apartment. His landlord is not easily charmed and refuses to give his tenant a break on rent. Giorgio looks forward to the day the old geezer dies, and he will deal with his widow. With enough flattery she will offer him the place at a reasonable price.

Sophie occupies his thoughts. She is the most talented stylist on his team. Her personality endears her to clients. The others are all good, but Sophie is great. Giorgio requires his staff to be female. He does not want good-looking men cramping his style. He does not care that it is discrimination. Sophie ignores him every time he mentions a new contract. Unless she plans to leave town, there is no other salon in the city to compare with Casa di Giorgio. Her contract ran out at midnight. He made a mistake by letting her leave today without signing a new one.

He walked the two flights to his apartment, happy to be alone tonight. Though proud of his prowess with women, even Casanova needed a break now and then.

There was soft music coming from the apartment. His heart pounded in alarm when he opened the unlocked door.

"Hello, Hank, it has been a long time."

"Tammy Sue, what are you doing here? How did you find me?"

"You did not make it easy. You left no traces of Hank Henshaw behind. After all this time, I saved enough money to hire a private detective. He uncovered your identity and discovered your lucrative business here. Half the money belongs to the kids and me. I am here to collect it."

"Forget it, Tammy Sue; I am not giving you any of my hard-earned money. You will have to sue to get a dime from me and you cannot afford the attorney fees. Get out before I call the cops."

"I will get out, but I will not leave town. My attorney will not charge to represent me against my snake of a husband. You can kiss your fancy digs goodbye. You owe me five years of child support. The courts do not look kindly on fathers who abandon their children."

Tammy Sue retrieved her purse and walked out the door to the staircase. Giorgio stifled the urge to give her a slight push, ending the nightmare she had started.

* * *

Cynthia Brainard paced in the living room of her small house near downtown Brentwood. She knew Tammy Sue Henshaw had disregarded her advice to stay away from her husband after she had arrived in town.

Cynthia is an associate attorney at the Steven Gray Law Firm. Her parents, Victor and Rosemary Brainard instilled a sense of duty to help those less fortunate. At an early age, she learned not every child grew up in a loving and prosperous home.

When the local legal aid office referred an abandonment case to Steve Gray's office, Cynthia accepted it without hesitation. The woman, Tammy Sue Henshaw, and her two children were abandoned by her husband, Hank, five years ago. She and her children were forced to give up their modest home. They moved in with her aging parents. It took Tammy Sue a few years to save enough money to hire a private detective. Upon discovering Hank Henshaw's identity, he found that he goes by the name Giorgio and owns an upscale beauty parlor in Brentwood. The detective took pity on Tammy Sue and encouraged her to contact legal aid. It irked the detective that the deadbeat husband and father drove around town in a fancy sports car and owned a successful business.

Cynthia knew Giorgio by reputation and from the salon. She and her mother marveled at how women fell for the man's charm. Giorgio's charm was wasted on the attractive Rosemary and her daughter. He never pushed after he was rebuffed. Other women enjoyed the attention and were overly generous with their tips.

* * *

Tammy Sue was barely twenty when she met Hank Henshaw. She fell in love with the thirty-year-old charmer. A sweet young country girl was the last person Hank intended to marry. When Tammy Sue discovered she was in the family way, her father changed Hank's mind about marriage. He settled down with a job in construction. He dreamt of being a carefree bachelor and after two children, he found a way out. If he ever regretted his decision, it never showed.

* * *

Cynthia encouraged Tammy Sue to visit Brentwood after the holidays, where they would decide on the best course of action. Arrangements were made for Tammy Sue to stay in the Brentwood Hotel. Tammy Sue left her children with her parents and drove to Brentwood on New Year's Eve. Any love she had for her husband disappeared as he had. She did not care about money for herself but wanted her children to have the advantages she could ill afford.

The private detective had given her Hank's address. When she arrived, she knocked on the door. There was no answer. Years ago, Hank showed her how to jimmy a lock. She was able to open the door and waited for him to arrive.

He arrived wearing a ridiculous purple velvet tuxedo. His hair and well-groomed beard were darker than Tammy Sue remembered. She fought the urge to giggle when she realized his hair was dyed.

Giorgio had had enough and rushed his wife out the door. He never asked about his children. What kind of man did she marry? Cynthia suggested Tammy Sue not try to see Hank on her own. After New Year's Day, a meeting would be arranged. Why hadn't she listened to the attorney?

Seeing the man who was now a stranger made her feel wretched.

* * *

It was well after midnight, and the revelers were still welcoming the new year as Tammy Sue walked the two blocks from Casa di Giorgio to the Brentwood Hotel.

Feeling restless and missing her two children, she had wandered earlier to the beauty salon owned by her husband. Curiosity made her climb the stairs leading to Hank's apartment. It was simple to pry open the lock and walk in. She knew it was a mistake but could not help herself. As she gazed at the lavish dwelling, her resentment of the man she had once loved increased.

It hurt that he had not asked about his children. When Hank last saw Timothy and Melissa, they were babies. Her earlier encounter with the cold-hearted man had left her wondering how he could have so easily fooled her.

It was a difficult night for Tammy Sue as she cried herself to sleep.

Chapter Five

Sophie awoke to feel a sense of freedom after five years of being under Giorgio's control. She dreads a confrontation with him about her plans to open her own shop. *I am being foolish. The man cannot stop me from following my dream.*

Meredith Donovan assured her everything is in order with her business loan. Sophie's Salon will be open within the month. Her head is swimming with ideas for the décor. Unlike Casa di Giorgio, Sophie's goal is to provide a comfortable, elegant environment. There will be no gilded mirrors hanging from the walls.

Stepping out of the shower, Sophie heard her phone; she hastily picked up, hoping it was Travis.

"I hope I didn't wake you."

"I've been up for hours," she giggled.

"Are we still on for today? I saw where the Brentwood Hotel is serving a champagne brunch."

"Nothing like starting the new year with a bit of the bubbly. I would love to celebrate my freedom from Giorgio in style."

"I will pick you up in twenty minutes. Will that give you enough time?"

"I'll be ready," Sophie said, knowing she would have to hustle.

Travis smiled; he had wondered if the glow from being with her would wear off this morning; it had not. He is eager to see her again. Could he have fallen in love after only one night together? Until he met Sophie, he had not believed it was possible.

* * *

Tammy Sue awoke to the sound of her cell phone after a restless night.

"Did I wake you, Tammy Sue?"

Tammy Sue lied, claiming she was not sleeping. "I hope you are not angry with me, Cynthia. I ignored your warning and saw Hank last night."

"I am not angry. I would have done the same. Did he make it difficult for you?"

"Our meeting was brief. Any lingering feelings I had for the man had disappeared. He never even asked about his children."

Cynthia did not like the idea of Tammy Sue being alone in a strange city on a holiday. She invited her to her parents' home for their annual New Year's Day luncheon.

"I cannot impose on your family. I have a book to read, and the exercise room is calling my name."

"It sounds perfectly dreadful. My mother will have my head if I allow you to spend the day alone. I will be by in an hour."

Tammy Sue was not looking forward to spending the day alone thinking about tomorrow when she will meet with a judge to discuss child support. Cynthia said the court would be on her side. She wants no money for herself, only her children. It did not matter that they wore hand-me-downs when they were babies. Tammy Sue fears they will be ridiculed if they wear shabby clothes now that they are in school.

* * *

Jessica watches as Rick shows off his cooking skills with ham and cheese omelets. The detective in him reads the worry on Jessica's face.

"You are worried about Sophie, aren't you?" he asks as he serves her breakfast.

"I have a bad feeling about Giorgio. He is not to be trusted. He has taken advantage of Sophie for years, and I cannot see him letting her go without a fight. Meredith thinks her new venture will go through without a hitch. I hope she is right."

Rick watched Giorgio at the New Year's Eve party. He seemed to zero in on the wealthiest women, no matter their age. Rick can spot a phony, and the name Giorgio is not the only fake thing about the guy. He backed away from Olivia Talbot when Reggie Talbot glared at him. When Reggie is displeased, the recipient of his anger better beware.

Rick enjoyed Sophie's company last night. He agreed with Jessica that she and Travis Bloom were a good match. Travis deserves some happiness in his life. People tend to back away from him when they hear his father is, alleged gangster, Harry Bloom.

"Sophie is allowed to open her own business. There should be room for two upscale beauty parlors in a city the size of Brentwood."

"They are hairstylists, not hairdressers, and we call them salons. I hope Giorgio feels the same. The problem is the stylists employed by Giorgio will want to join Sophie. Giorgio is not well-liked by his staff. He could be vindictive if he loses business."

"Should I think about having my hair styled? I will try Sophie to help support her business when it opens."

"She is planning a grand opening party when the redecorating is complete. She told me purple would be nowhere in sight."

"You mean the purple tux was only the beginning?"

"Oh yes, he has purple walls, purple chairs, purple towels, and the stylists all wear purple smocks. The hair dryers and curling irons are all purple as well."

* * *

Cynthia said Tammy Sue's surprise visit to Giorgio had not caused any harm. Breaking and entering could be a problem, but the lawyer doubted Giorgio would press charges. His abandonment of his wife and children has already gotten him in trouble.

A client of Giorgio's, Meredith Donavan, is an attorney. He dials her number after searching for it. *I do not care if it is a holiday. This is an emergency.*

Meredith listens to Giorgio's plea for legal advice. Giorgio, has this woman threatened you with bodily harm?"

"No, Tammy Sue would not hurt a fly. She is after my money. I must stop her."

"If you are not physically in danger, there is nothing we can do today. I suggest you relax; watch a movie or some football on television. Call my office in the morning. We will discuss your situation."

"She has herself a lawyer already. You can bet they have a plan to cheat me out of my money, and it will be all your fault."

"Giorgio, I am late for an engagement today. We will talk in the morning." Meredith hangs up before he can argue with her.

Chapter Six

The stupid broad hung up on me. I do not have a choice; I must wait until Miss High and Mighty is ready to help me. Giorgio heard people talking about a brunch at the Brentwood Hotel. It is a suitable place to schmooze with the wealthy old ladies and fill his empty belly. A day spent watching football does not appeal to him.

* * *

Sophie changes clothes three times, hoping to find something suitable for the most high-class hotel in the city. Travis's knock on the door forces her to decide. The look on his face tells her it was an excellent choice.

"You look terrific, Sophie, better than last night, if that is possible." He gave her a kiss on the cheek.

"You look good yourself," she said with a smile.

Sophie feels her heart beating faster as he drives to the hotel. She tells herself she is looking for heartache if she falls too quickly for this man. Travis is not in her league despite what he said.

When they arrive at the hotel, they are seated in the restaurant. The aromas coming from the buffet are tantalizing. After a few sips of champagne, they walk to the buffet to fill their plates.

Sophie's eyes go directly to the dessert table. She has never seen an array of delectable items such as this. "Travis, my mother would not approve, but I'm tempted to have dessert first."

Travis laughs. He, too, has a sweet tooth. "It sounds tempting, but the roast beef is calling my name. It is a holiday, and you are allowed to eat your meal in any order you wish."

Sophie examines the wide variety of dishes. The truth is, she adores food. "I'll save room for dessert," she says as she fills her plate.

Although stuffed after the meal, Sophie and Travis fill their dessert plates with a selection of treats to share.

From across the room, Harry Bloom watches as his son and a girl giggle like school children while filling their mouths with food. Harry nudges his wife, Sylvia. "Your son is with a pretty girl. She looks nothing like the pasty-faced babes you try to pawn off on him."

"Is Travis here? I do not see him."

"Put your glasses on. He is sitting across the room."

Though Sylvia is nearing sixty, she refuses to wear her glasses in public for fear they make her look old. Harry tells her she looks old because she is old, but she ignores his insult. Their marriage is not typical. Harry always has a mistress on the side. Sylvia does not care as long as she has unlimited charging power and does what she pleases. They are seldom seen together; today is an exception. Harry insists they spend Christmas and New Year's Day together. For the rest of the year, Sylvia is on her own.

As a child, Travis was cared for by the Bloom handyman and housekeeper. What the young boy knew about a loving relationship came from Mr. and Mrs. Cooper. He loved the old couple and still visits them often in their retirement home.

* * *

Giorgio walks in the door. He complains about the excessive cost of the meal. The hostess suggests he might prefer the coffee shop instead. He gives her a chilling scowl.

As he fills his plate with the items, he considers the most expensive, he spots Sophia sitting with the guy from last night. He cannot understand why she is smiling. As of midnight, she was unemployed. He would refuse to offer her a new contract if she were not of value to him. He puts his plate down and walks to her table, helping himself to a sip of her champagne.

"Go back to your table, Buddy. Take the champagne with you." Travis signaled the waiter to bring Sophie a new glass.

Giorgio can tell by this guy's demeanor and expensive clothes; he comes from money. "Did Sophie tell you she is a hairstylist?"

"What is your point, buddy?"

"I am not your buddy; stop calling me that." Giorgio's voice rose an octave in frustration.

Before he could take a breath, two large men stood on either side of him. Each held an arm, and they lifted him off the floor as they casually walked to the door.

"Put me down. I have not eaten my food."

The two men disappeared after giving Giorgio a warning look. He knew it was best to walk away without going back for his food.

Sophie looks at Travis in disbelief.

"I am sorry, Sophie. Those two are my father's henchmen. He is sitting across the room with my mother. If I had known they would be here, I would never have suggested this place."

"They are not going to kill Giorgio, are they?"

"No, killing is a last resort, even for my old man. He and mother dearest are on their way over to our table."

"Happy New Year, son. Are you going to introduce me to your little filly?"

"The little filly is Sophie Clark. Sophie, my parents, Harry and Sylvia. Was that exhibition necessary, Father?"

"The weasel got in your face; I could not let him get away with it. I will always have your back, whether you like it or not."

"Sophie Clark. Is your father Walter Clark, president of the bank? I did not know that old codger had a sweet young daughter."

"No, Mr. Bloom, I am not a native of Brentwood. I am a hairstylist at Casa di Giorgio. Mrs. Bloom, your hair looks lovely."

"Yes, dear. I have it done at an exclusive salon in New York City."

"Thanks for stopping by our table. Enjoy your meal and Happy New Year."

Sylvia wanted to question her son about his choice of a luncheon partner, but Harry pulled her away. Travis did not hide his disapproval of his parents' lifestyle. It was better to depart than air the family's grievances in public.

Travis fears the encounter with his parents will ruin their budding romance. "I'm sorry about the interruption; I never dreamt my father would choose this place to be seen with my mother."

"If you had not told me he was a gangster, I would never have guessed. He is a charming man."

"He was on his good behavior. He is not a man who can be trusted. I will say I prefer him to my snob of a mother. She and Giorgio would make a good pair. They are both phonies."

"I'm sorry your childhood was not a happy one."

"It was not bad at all. Mr. and Mrs. Cooper, the caregivers, were like parents to me. They gave me the love and attention I never got from my parents. I had plenty of friends while in elementary school. The mansion had everything a kid could want. A bowling alley, two pools, a movie theater, and tennis and volleyball courts. I was the most popular kid in my class. When some parents discovered who my father was, they forbade their children to come to my house. They changed their tune when Mr. and Mrs. Cooper assured them it was a healthy environment, and Harry Bloom was seldom at home. After law school, I planned to leave Brentwood to get away from the stigma of being a Bloom. Instead, I chose to stay and work to bring honor to the name. The majority of my clients are those who cannot fight for themselves. I want to give back to society what my father has taken away. Does that make sense?"

"It makes perfect sense."

Chapter Seven

Still fuming over his experience at the hotel, Giorgio drives to Mindy's apartment to ask who Sophie is romancing these days.

"Mindy, open the door. I know you are in there."

"Giorgio, what do you want? It is a holiday; the shop is closed."

"I am not here to take you to the salon. I want to ask you a question."

Mindy is not surprised when Giorgio asks about Travis. She is happy her friend is with him again today. Sophie deserves some happiness after dealing with Giorgio. Mindy tells him the man's name is Travis Bloom. "He is a lawyer and the son of Harry Bloom."

"The notorious gangster, Harry Bloom? Why is he interested in Sophie; he could get any girl he wanted?"

"He does not want any girl; he wants Sophie. It is great."

Now Giorgio understands why those two goons picked on him. The relationship will not last. Sophie is a goody-two-shoes; she will never accept Harry Bloom's son in her life.

Giorgio's stomach growls. He asks Mindy what she has in her refrigerator. Bloom's flunkies prevented him from eating his meal.

"Giorgio, I am not on the clock. If you are hungry, there is a hamburger joint down the street. Let me get back to my movie. I will see you tomorrow."

Mindy could be read like a book. Giorgio had the feeling she was hiding something. He would get it out of her if he had to hang around all day.

"I would not mind seeing this movie. Scoot over, let me sit next to you while you tell me your secret."

Easily intimidated, Mindy revealed Sophie's plans to open her own salon.

"Where would Sophie get the money? She is involved with Harry Bloom's son. Is that criminal funding for her? Did Harry Bloom give her the money to start her own business?"

"No, Harry Bloom has nothing to do with it. Sophie used her inheritance from her grandfather. She has been planning this since he died four years ago. She was bound by the contract she signed with you. Now, she is free to do as she pleases."

Mindy covered her mouth. What made her blurt that out? Sophie will be furious with her.

Giorgio charged out the door. He had not seen this coming; he assumed Sophie would sign a new contract in the morning. *There must be a way to stop her from stealing my clients. I cannot let her get away with it.*

He drove past the burger joint and onto the bar a block away. It is less than twenty-four hours into the new year, and his world is shattering. Tammy Sue tracked him down, and his best stylist has plans to leave him.

* * *

The annual New Year's Day luncheon at the Brainard home is underway with family and friends. Cynthia arrives at her parents' home with a nervous Tammy Sue Henshaw.

Rosemary Brainard welcomes Tammy Sue, putting her at ease. She is greeted with warm smiles by the other guests. Cynthia introduces her as a friend visiting from out-of-town.

Meredith pulls Cynthia aside. "I understand you have taken a legal aid referral. Is your friend your new client?"

"She is, I didn't want her to be alone in a hotel room on a holiday."

"I had a call from Giorgio earlier. He wants me to represent him against harassment from a young woman named Tammy Sue."

"That young woman is the wife he abandoned five years ago. Giorgio's real name is Hank Henshaw; he is the father of her two children. Tammy Sue lives with her elderly parents and her children. She saved the money to hire a private detective who tracked him down. Tammy Sue confronted him, and he showed no signs of cooperating. We are meeting with Judge Redding tomorrow morning. The judge has no tolerance for deadbeat dads."

"It would be a conflict of interest to represent the loathsome man. I will recommend another firm. If I can do anything to help the woman, let me know." Meredith felt relief at not having to deal with Giorgio.

* * *

After overeating at the brunch buffet, Sophie and Travis take a walk in Chelsea Gardens. The sun is shining, and the air is crisp on a pleasant winter day. The shrubs and dormant flower beds are covered in snow. Children and adults ice skate on the frozen pond. Travis buys two cups of steaming hot chocolate from a street vendor. The couple sits on a bench, watching the skaters. Sophie has never felt so relaxed. Her phone rings, drawing her back to reality.

"Mindy, what is up? I thought you planned to watch movies all day."

"That was my plan until Giorgio stopped by." Sophie hears her sobs.

"What did he do to you? Did he hurt you?"

"No, he did not hurt me. You are going to kill me. I do not know how he made me tell him you are leaving to start your own shop."

"I will not kill you, Mindy. You saved me from springing it on him tomorrow."

"He is mad, Sophie. He left, slamming the door so hard the walls shook."

"He will calm down. I will talk to him tomorrow. Go back to your movie, and do not worry."

Chapter Eight

Jessica arrives at the law office early the following morning. Meredith is already sitting at her desk.

"I thought I was early; you must have been up in the wee hours."

"I worried whether everything is in order for Sophie's new salon. We missed you at the Brainard's yesterday; Rosemary and Victor organized a lovely party, as always."

"I am sorry I missed it. Rick was on duty all day, and I was busy with rewrites. What did I miss besides a wonderful spread and good company?"

"Cynthia brought her client, a young woman named Tammy Sue Henshaw. Tammy Sue is the wife, Hank Henshaw abandoned over five years ago."

"The name doesn't sound familiar, should it?"

"He is known in Brentwood as Giorgio. The rat left Tammy Sue with two children to support. Cynthia has taken her case. Giorgio will be sued for child support."

"I always knew that guy was a piece of work. Cynthia better prepare for a fight; from what I have heard of Giorgio; he does not like to part with money. I am glad Sophie is finally out of his web. The others will follow her lead and distance themselves from the charlatan."

"Giorgio called me yesterday complaining that some woman was harassing him. I told him to call me during business hours. As it turns out, he is married to the woman Cynthia is representing. Of course, I cannot advise him on the matter."

* * *

Giorgio wakes with a throbbing head. An empty bottle of whiskey is beside his bed. It is not like him to tie one on like he did. He always tries to keep his head clear. He recalls Tammy Sue sitting on his sofa when he arrived home from the New Year's Eve party. *She is still a knock-out. It is unfortunate she had to get herself pregnant.* He never wanted kids, and she stuck him with two. He did what he had to do; he walked out and started a new life for himself. Unexpectedly, she pops back into his life and wants money. *Well, she is not getting any from him.*

Giorgio splashes water on his face and picks up his phone to call Meredith Donovan. *She had better not put me off again today; I will have her disbarred.*

"Hello, Giorgio. You did not tell me you are legally married to the woman you say is harassing you. Mrs. Henshaw is a client of an associate in my office. I am unable to discuss the matter further or offer legal advice. I will give you the name of another lawyer to call."

"Tammy Sue is a charity case; I am not one. You women all stick together. I should have called a male attorney in the first place." He slammed the phone down.

Meredith opened her door to see an anxious Sophie standing there.

"I am sorry, Sophie. I needed to take that annoying phone call. Are you ready to sign the papers making you the new owner of Sophie's Salon?"

"I have been ready for years. I do not know why I am so nervous."

"It is a big step, but you are ready for this. I have no doubt you will be successful."

"Have you told Giorgio your news?"

"Mindy took care of that for me. He intimidated her into blurting it out. It saves me from his wrath. I do not feel I need to explain myself to him."

Jessica has a sinking feeling in the pit of her stomach. Giorgio's world is falling apart, and he is not the type to go down without a fight. She hopes she is wrong.

"I cleared my morning schedule. Would you like Jessica and me to accompany you to your new salon?"

"I'd love it if you would come with me."

"Is there room for one more?" Travis asks from the doorway.

Jessica and Meredith smile when they see the loving looks these two share. After walking the block from the law office to the shop. Sophie unlocks the front door.

"I had forgotten how much work needs to be done before I can get it looking like a beauty salon. How are you with a paintbrush, Travis?"

"What is a paintbrush?" He asks, joking. "We can put my father's henchmen to work. Gonzo is so tall, he does not need a stepladder."

"Since they follow you anyway, they might as well do something useful."

Sophie had dreamed of this place for so long, that she described the furnishings and colors in detail. She wanted to be sure the sale went through before she contacted a renovation company.

Travis made a phone call. "The renovators will be here in twenty minutes to give you an estimate. If you do not like their prices or ideas, we will try another."

Sophia looked at Travis skeptically.

"Do not worry. This company has nothing to do with my father. The owner is Ron Hammond. He is an old classmate who took over his dad's business. The company has a good reputation, and Ron is a great guy."

"Ron's company remodeled my dad's study," said Jessica. "He did a terrific job at a reasonable price."

While waiting for Ron, they walked to the second floor. Sophie envisioned a fully equipped day spa. For now, a hair and nail salon will be enough.

* * *

When Ron arrived, Sophie walked with him and pointed to where she wanted the equipment. He made a few suggestions but mostly agreed with her. Ron walked through the space, measuring walls, floors, and rooms. He jotted numbers on his pad, brought out his calculator, and gave her an estimate before he left.

"You will want to get another estimate to compare. That is understandable. I will wait to hear from you."

"I do not need another estimate. You did not argue with my ideas. I would like to hire you if you want the job."

* * *

Giorgio walked by Sophie's new shop on his way to the law offices of Black and Evans. After raising a fuss, Hollister Black agreed to see the man, if only to shut him up. Giorgio peeked in the window. *What a mess, I will not worry about the competition. This place will not be open for business for six months or more.* A smile crossed his face. He felt better than he had all day. Sophie is on her way to bankruptcy, and Tammy Sue will be on her way home to the two brats without a penny of his money.

Chapter Nine

Hollister Black sat at his desk as Giorgio bemoaned the sudden appearance of his estranged wife. An upstanding member of the community and an ardent family man, he has no compassion for a father who abandons his wife and children.

"You are no more a Giorgio than I am. Tell me what your legal name is before you proceed."

"As if it matters. My name is Hank Henshaw. I prefer to be called Giorgio."

"I prefer to be called George Clooney, Mr. Henshaw, but I am still Hollister Black. Let us stick to the truth, shall we? Why did you leave your wife and children? Were you knocked unconscious and robbed of your memory?"

"That's it! I was knocked over the head and could not remember a thing. I started a new life; now that I have a few bucks, my wife is after me for my money."

"Mr. Henshaw, I don't' believe a word you say. Unless you tell me the truth, I cannot help you."

Giorgio had no choice. He told Mr. Black his version of the story. Tammy Sue and the kids stifled him, so he left. Also, he doubted the kids were his; she liked other men. "Any one of them could have fathered her brats."

"A simple test will prove paternity. If the children are yours, there is nothing I can do for you. I do not represent deadbeat dads."

Giorgio knew he had not fooled the lawyer. He spewed profanities as he stomped from the office.

Casa di Giorgio had been open for two hours. Though his head still throbbed, he knew he must make an appearance at the salon.

A hush came over the shop when he appeared. Sophie's chair remained empty. Her appointment log showed no bookings. Some of her regulars were scheduled with other stylists. It occurred to him that his girls knew Sophie's plans and neglected to share them with him.

Giorgio was about to throw a fit when he heard someone call his name.

Turning around, he saw Olivia Talbot smiling at him.

"Olivia, my favorite customer." The day was looking better.

* * *

Judge Angela Redding did her best to put Tammy Sue Henshaw at ease. Tammy Sue's story was like many she had heard in her years as a family court judge. Cynthia had told her to bring the children's birth certificates to the meeting. Hank Henshaw was listed as the children's father. Though legally, it was enough to prove Mr. Henshaw believed he was the father, the judge ordered a paternity test.

"Judge, Hank will never agree to a test."

If he refuses, he will be in contempt of court and will face jail time and fines. He will be ordered to pay child support. I have been to Casa di Giorgio. It is a popular salon. He is not a pauper."

"I only need enough to buy my children nice clothes and pay for activities their friends enjoy."

"Your son and daughter deserve to have the simple things most children take for granted. If your husband refuses to take responsibility for their expenses, the court will see that he does. Mrs. Henshaw, go home to your children. I will start the ball rolling. If Mr. Henshaw agrees to the paternity test, we will arrange for a cheek swab for the children. Your attorney will keep you informed of the next step."

Cynthia drove Tammy Sue to the train station. Her gratitude was evident in the hug she gave her attorney.

* * *

Ron Hammond promises to begin designing the salon's interior. Sophie has a vision of what she wants, which is helpful. Her enthusiasm inspires Ron to give the project his undivided attention, so the renovation can begin.

* * *

Jessica and Meredith returned to the law office. Cynthia fills them in on Tammy Sue Henshaw's meeting with Judge Redding. It was no surprise the judge sided with Tammy Sue. Children were always favored over a derelict father. Jessica is relieved Tammy Sue is on her way home. Giorgio could react badly if his lifestyle is threatened,

* * *

The last thing on Giorgio's mind is Tammy Sue and the children. He is busy fawning over Olivia Talbot.

"Giorgio, I am a golf widow this weekend. My husband is playing in a tournament in Arizona. If you have no plans, will you stop by my house to tweak my hair this evening? I will make it worth your while."

"I'm as free as a bird; it will be my pleasure to give you my special treatment."

When Marian Ballard overheard the conversation, she turned green with envy. She had a crush on Giorgio. Although she cannot compete with Olivia, she will make sure Reggie hears about her seduction of Giorgio.

Chapter Ten

The following morning, Giorgio left the Talbot home with a smile and a few crisp hundred-dollar bills in his pocket. *Olivia's charms are wasted on old man Talbot.*

From her bedroom window, Olivia watches him. *The man knows his way around a woman. I do not mind sharing Reggie's money with him; Giorgio is worth it.* She brushes aside thoughts of last night as she dresses for her meeting with the First Community Church ladies auxiliary.

* * *

Ron Hammond slept briefly after working into the night. Sophie's excitement over her new shop prompted him to finish the blueprint before the light of day. If she approves the plans, work will begin soon.

Sophie had trouble falling asleep the night before. The ideas for the shop and fears of what could go wrong filled her head. She had avoided seeing Giorgio yesterday but knew she could not put it off any longer. The ringing of her phone startled her.

"Sophie, I hope I did not wake you. The blueprints are ready for you to review. I can meet you at the shop within the hour."

Sophie had a quick shower, dressed, and was out the door. Travis called as she drove to the empty building.

"Travis, I would love it if you would meet Ron and me at the shop. I am so excited I cannot think straight. I need a pair of neutral eyes."

"I am on my way. Jessica just arrived; I will bring her along. The boss's daughter is allowed to play hooky for a friend."

* * *

Sophie knows her dream will come true when she sees Ron's sketches. She and the others cannot find anything that needs to be changed in his plans. Ron and Travis help her choose a contractor for the renovation.

Her sense of euphoria dwindles as she drives to Casa di Giorgio to face her former employer. A hush comes over the salon when Sophie walks through the door. She guesses she has been the topic of conversation since the day before. Her voice cracks as she asks if Giorgio is in his office. After five years in the salon, she feels like a stranger.

Her empty station serves as a reminder of what she is risking by going off on her own.

Mindy catches her eye, whispering that Giorgio is in a good mood today. She and the other stylists believe Olivia Talbot is the reason. Sophie rolls her eyes, wondering what Giorgio will do if Reggie Talbot suspects hanky-panky is going on with his wife.

"Well, well, well! The rebellious child returns to the fold."

"I am here to say goodbye to you and the staff. My new salon will open soon. I hope we can be friendly competitors."

"You expect to succeed in that dump you call a salon. That is a laugh. You would be better off burning it down and collecting the insurance money. I have your contract ready. If you sign it today, we will continue as if yesterday never happened."

"You did not hear me, Giorgio. That dump is the new Sophie's Salon. It will be open for business very soon. Do not expect an invitation to the grand opening."

Giorgio's fake smile turns to fury. Sophie feels a chill pass through her. She walks out of his office. With one last glance at her former station, she waves goodbye to the other stylists. "I hope to see everyone soon." They all smile, hoping to be free of Giorgio's control before long.

* * *

"How did your meeting with Giorgio go?" Travis asked when they met for lunch.

"As expected, I ruined his good mood. According to Mindy, Olivia Talbot was the reason for his cheerfulness before I showed up. He called my new place a dump. It makes me wonder if he checked it out yesterday. The man is not going to make it easy for me."

"I can always call Gonzo if he gives you any trouble."

"Do not joke about your father's henchmen. Those guys give me the creeps."

Travis is sorry he called attention to his father. His connection to Harry Bloom is something Sophie tries to ignore.

* * *

Jessica stops Cynthia in the hallway. “Are there any developments in Tammy Sue's case against Giorgio?"

"He is being served with a court order today. He will undoubtedly ignore it, and then the fun begins. Judge Redding is vehement about making him own up to his responsibilities. His charm will not work on her.”

“I’d love to be a fly on the wall when he is served.”

“Me too,” Cynthia chuckles.

* * *

Mindy watches as the serious-looking man walks through the doors of the salon. He asks for Hank Henshaw.

“There is no one here by that name, sir.”

He looks at his notes, and says, “Giorgio.”

Mindy knocks on Giorgio’s door. He shouts for her to go away.

“There is someone here to see you. He will not leave until you talk to him.”

Giorgio throws open the door, his face beet red. "Who wants to see me?"

The man verifies the name Hank Henshaw aka Giorgio, hands him the order, and leaves.

Giorgio reads the order for a paternity test. He has not a chance to wriggle out of having to support Tammy Sue's brats. He will refuse the test but knows they will get him eventually. What else could go wrong? His girls will walk out on him as soon as their contracts expire. Sophie will take them in. It was her plan all along to ruin him. *She will pay for her disloyalty. I will make sure of it.*

Chapter Eleven

The renovations at Sophie's Salon transformed the shop into an elegant yet welcoming environment. She is ready for the grand opening of her new salon. Sophie is the only stylist, but there is room for several others in the coming weeks and months. When Mindy Lawrence's contract with Giorgio expires, she will be the first to join her friend.

Giorgio has hired several recent graduates to replace the stylists who will leave for Sophie's Salon. Since Sophie only provides hair and nail services, Giorgio has hired a young male masseuse to attract some women. Most of the salon's clients say they will follow their favorite stylist to Sophie's Salon.

Jessica, Meredith, and Cynthia arrive at the new salon to help Sophie set up for the festivities.

"You are all so supportive of me. I have visions of standing alone in my shop, drinking champagne by myself."

Travis walked through the door. "Is my best girl doubting herself? You will have so many people here tonight, that they will need to take a number to enter. The office is abuzz about the party tonight.

Even Mrs. Peabody is looking forward to kicking up her heels."

Meredith laughed. "We had better have a wheelchair handy."

"Mrs. Peabody has been around since I was a kid," said Jessica. "She seemed old back then. When Natalie and I visited dad at the office, our first stop was Mrs. Peabody's candy jar. She could have retired years ago, but the law firm is her life.

"Hey, as long as she keeps handing out paychecks with that candy, I hope she never leaves."

A smile spread across Sophie's face when she heard Travis's words. He had never had to worry about a paycheck in his life. Despite his father's dubious business practices, Harry Bloom supported his family. Travis has an honorable profession defending those who need his help, instead of living off his father's money. It is one of the many things she loves about him.

* * *

The open house is scheduled for early evening. The friends will gather later to help Sophia welcome her guests.

Cynthia meets Tammy Sue Henshaw at the train station. She returns to Brentwood for a meeting with Judge Redding and Giorgio. As a result of his stalling tactics, the judge ordered him to appear before her or face jail time. He has no choice but to comply.

"Tammy Sue, you will be in court tomorrow as an observer. The judge will manage Giorgio. She is accustomed to men like him in her profession. What you are asking for is fair to you and the children. Come with me tonight to a grand opening here in town. You will drive yourself crazy if you sit in your hotel room alone tonight. Giorgio's former hair stylist has opened her own shop. Giorgio will not be at the party. His name is not on the guest list."

* * *

"Reggie, why do you insist on attending the opening of a hair salon destined to fail. The upstart will never compete with Casa di Giorgio."

"My interest has nothing to do with the salon. The owner is Travis Bloom's girlfriend. Harry Bloom has taken a liking to the girl and suggested I attend the foolish event. Harry's suggestions are not to be taken lightly. If he wants me there, that is where I will be. You and your effusive charm will be by my side. I am late for a meeting at the club. Be ready to go when I return."

Olivia has no choice but to attend the opening. Giorgio is furious with his girl Sophie for leaving him to open her own place. How will she explain when Reggie gives an order, that she must comply or face the consequences. She dials his private number.

Giorgio listens as Olivia explains Reggie's insistence that she attends the opening.

"I am thinking of a plan to kill two birds with one stone. Wait for my call." Giorgio ended the call before Olivia could say another word.

Giorgio held the bottle of cyanide in his hand. The stuff would put an end to Sophie's plan to ruin him. His problem was how to get her to ingest it without her knowing. They could meet for happy hour, and he would spike her drink. It would not work; he would be the prime suspect in her murder. He and Olivia had kept their relationship quiet. No one knew she was cheating on her husband. They had talked about running off together, but both were fond of money and the idea of living on love was beyond them. With old Reggie out of the way, Olivia would have all the money they would need. The grand opening is the perfect setting. Reggie would die and Sophie's new place would become a murder scene. She will be ruined before she gives her first shampoo. He and Olivia will quietly slip away. That greedy Tammy Sue will be out of luck when she cannot find him to bilk him for his money.

Olivia met Giorgio in his office at the salon. The staff was gone, they were alone. Giorgio, do you think you can pull it off? I will be the prime suspect. I want to be rid of Reggie, but I do not want to go to prison."

"This stuff acts quickly. You will be on the opposite side of the room yakking it up with your girlfriends. As far as anyone is concerned, I have never met Reggie and you are just another client. After the funeral, you will feel the need to get away from your memories of the old boy. We will meet on some island in the Caribbean and live happily ever after."

"It sounds wonderful. Who will take the blame for Reggie's demise?"

"No one. It will look like an accident and Sophie will be held responsible for her carelessness."

"I must pick out a special dress to wear tonight. I can hardly wait to play the grieving widow."

"I cannot wait to see your performance.

Chapter Twelve

Tears filled Sophie's eyes as she stood back to admire her new salon. The caterers placed the last of the champagne glasses on the table and an assortment of tempting appetizers. Daisy arrangements graced the main table, and smaller vases of the spring flowers were placed on several tabletops, where the guests could sit and enjoy the company of their friends and neighbors.

"Travis, I could not have done this without your help. You, Meredith, and Jessica made my dream come true long before I thought possible."

"We helped you, but this venture is all yours, Sophie. You never gave up on your dream. I love you for your determination and for being you."

"I had better get dressed before the guests arrive. Though I am comfortable in jeans and a sweatshirt, it is not the image I want to project."

Sophie planned to change into her new dress in her office since time was of the essence.

While he waited, Travis glanced around the salon. Though Ron and his crew's renovations are exceptional, it all started with Sophie's dream.

Sophie trembled as she applied her makeup. She calmed herself by thinking of Travis and how much she loved him. She wanted to look like a serious, sophisticated entrepreneur. Had she picked the wrong dress? Is it too casual? Did she make the wrong choice? Her shoes pinched her toes. Did she need a bigger size? Was her hair too curly or not curly enough? She stepped out of her office to see Travis smiling at her.

"You look like a successful business owner. Your dress is perfect for the occasion. You are truly a vision from head to toe."

Travis always knew the right thing to say.

* * *

The guests began to arrive. Most were familiar to Sophie; she called them by name and introduced herself to the others. They all wished her success with the new salon and marveled at the transformation of the old fabric shop.

Reggie Talbot arrived with Olivia on his arm. Sophie recognized Olivia from Giorgio's place. She could not understand what interest Reggie would have in her salon. He surely had a barber on staff to cut and style his hair.

Reggie nodded to Sophie, saying nothing. Instead, he spoke to Travis. "Young man, be sure to mention my presence to your father."

Travis knew Harry Bloom had somehow coerced Talbot to attend the open house. It meant only one thing; Harry would not be attending. His presence would distract from Sophie's party. His dirty dealings were well known in Brentwood. He was either feared or loathed or both.

* * *

Jessica could not help but stare at Olivia Talbot. Her full-length, form-fitting gown had a slit up the side that ended at her panty line. That is if she was wearing panties at all. The bodice barely covered her ample bosom.

"Olivia is advertising it tonight," said Rick.

"It makes you wonder who she is dressing for. I doubt it is for her husband. She is looking for someone."

At that moment, Giorgio entered the salon. He searched the room. His eyes landed on Olivia, and she looked longingly in his direction.

"Why is Giorgio here? Certainly not to wish Sophie well. It would be just like him to cause a scene attempting to ruin Sophie's grand opening."

"The way he is ogling Olivia Talbot, I do not think his mind is on Sophie at the moment. If he shows any signs of trouble, I will bring out my badge."

***

To avoid his gaze, Giorgio's stylists tried to remain hidden. For Mindy, it was too late. As he approached her, she cowered.

"Do not get any ideas, Mindy. There are still months left on your contract. If you think you will leave me for this dump, think again. Sophie's regulars belong to me. It is only a matter of time before she comes running back to Giorgio." He gave her a look that sent chills down her spine.

Tammy Sue stood next to Cynthia when Giorgio approached the two women.

"Where did you get the fancy duds, Tammy Sue? Are you spending my money already? You will not win in court when I tell the judge what a tramp you are. If you insist on continuing this frivolous lawsuit, you will force me to sue for custody of the brats. I will prove you are an unfit mother."

"Mr. Henshaw, I suggest you keep your mouth shut if you do not want me to announce your true identity. How many of your customers would continue to frequent Casa di Hank?"

Giorgio walked away, muttering under his breath. He caught Olivia's eye. She glanced toward the waiter who was distributing champagne to the guests. He felt for the bottle of cyanide he carried in his jacket pocket. The plan seemed simple when he had thought of it earlier. Slip the poison into Talbot's glass and be done with it. He and Olivia would be on their way to paradise with Talbot's money in their pocket. He will wait for a distraction and pour the cyanide into the man's champagne without being seen?

Suddenly, a screech was heard from across the room. It startled everyone within a few feet of Mrs. Peabody.

"Reginald Talbot, you old goat. I have not seen you in years. I am Elizabeth Crockett

Peabody. We attended high school together. You were the most likely to succeed. You lived up to the prognostication. I was voted the most likely to marry a rich man." Elizabeth laughed. "Instead, I married Hector Peabody. He was poor as a church mouse until the day he died."

The memory of his high school days came flooding back to Reggie. Those were the best years of his life. He remembered Elizabeth. Like most boys in the Class of '59, he had a crush on her.

"Elizabeth Crockett. You went to a secretarial school in New York City the last I heard. Here you are back in Brentwood. How long have you been in town?"

"After secretarial school, I returned home and married Hector. We were only married for ten years when a farming accident took him from me. Unfortunately, we had no children. After Hector died, I took my rusty skills and applied for a job at the Gray Law firm. Mr. Gray was just starting his practice back then. He keeps me on as a courtesy. If I did not have my job, I would have nothing."

"Olivia, find something or someone to keep you company. Elizabeth and I have much to talk about."

Reggie guided his old friend to the appetizer table. He handed her a glass of champagne and took one for himself.

"This is my opportunity. While the old woman distracts the old man, I will slip the poison into his drink."

Chapter Thirteen

Tammy Sue trembles after her encounter with Giorgio. Hank called our precious children brats. How could he say such a thing about his flesh and blood? I was a fool to fall for his charm when we first met. I am ashamed of my children's father."

"You have nothing to be ashamed of, Tammy Sue. Hank Henshaw is a poor excuse for a man. As with many troubled souls in this world, Hank lacks self-esteem. He is living a lie to make up for his failures. The man gave up on the only valuable thing in his life. He is to be pitied. You need not worry about him taking your children away from you. He will be laughed out of the courtroom if he tries."

Cynthia's words did little to calm Tammy Sue's fears. Throughout her life she has looked for the best in people. She cannot find any good in Hank. At this moment she hates him and wishes him dead.

* * *

Jessica tries to reassure Sophie she has nothing to fear from Giorgio. He came to her open house to intimidate her. Despite Giorgio's best efforts, Meredith assures the woman that her regulars will continue to follow her to her new salon. "We live in a free country, where women and men choose where to get their hair done. Giorgio knows most people here will leave his salon for yours."

""Most except for Mrs. Reggie Talbot. She is positively drooling as she watches Giorgio. Olivia is more than just a client at Casa di Giorgio," Jessica guesses.

"Reggie is ignoring his wife. Mrs. Peabody is distracting him. She has put a smile on the cantankerous old man's face."

"Mrs. Peabody is a dear. Mindy does her hair; she loves the old woman who reminds her of her grandmother. Look at Travis trying to persuade his father's goons to leave. I cannot believe Harry Bloom would send them. Those guys give me the creeps."

"It looks like he convinced them they were not needed. They are leaving. Travis is a great guy, no thanks to his parents. He is crazy about you, Sophie. You make a wonderful couple."

Sophie smiles, the party is going well. In another hour, the guests will be gone. After all her worry, the open house is a success. She looks forward to going home, kicking off her shoes, and spending the evening with Travis.

* * *

Reggie Talbot is enjoying spending time with his old friend, Elizabeth. He wonders when acquiring money and power took over his life. He did not have to prod his memory for the answer. He was a first-year student at the university. His friends convinced him to go to a sorority party. He balked at the idea. The sorority in question consisted of rich girls who walked around with their noses in the air. He would rather stay in his dorm and study. After being told they had plenty of beer, he changed his mind.

Reggie's instincts were right. Even after his second beer, he felt ill at ease. It was love at first sight when Pamela Ellington-Ross sashayed across the room directly to him.

"Why is a great-looking guy like you not dancing?" She took his hand and dragged him from his safe corner.

Pamela was the most beautiful girl he had ever seen. Her blonde hair and sparkling green eyes enticed him. He held her tightly as they danced, afraid she would slip away. Reggie had always been levelheaded. His mother often said he had been born a wise old man. One evening with Pamela and Reggie was no longer the rational young man he had always been.

For three months, his world revolved around Pamela. His studies suffered, and his grades plummeted. He was on the verge of losing his grant.

"Pamela, I want to marry you. I will quit school and get a job to support us."

"Reggie, what is this talk about marriage? We are having fun; why do you want to spoil it? I find you a pleasant diversion, but you do not fit in with my social circle. Now, stop all this talk about marriage and kiss me."

Reggie let out a gut-wrenching cry. Tears filled his eyes when he realized Pamela thought he was not good enough or rich enough for her. She laughed at his emotional reaction, telling him to grow up. Embarrassed by the tears streaming down his cheeks, Reggie turned and walked away from the woman he loved.

He indulged in his broken heart for several days. After the initial shock of Pamela's rejection, Reggie vowed to become a rich man and do what was necessary to make it happen.

After graduation, he founded his own real estate company with assistance from Harry Bloom. Though Reggie was known to cut corners, his organization shied away from criminal activity. Harry's loan had been paid in full many years before. Reggie knew he would never be free from Harry Bloom.

An impressive bank account did not bring the happiness Reggie envisioned. Through the years, he became a man of little joy. Building his wealth did not allow time for a personal life. At the age of sixty, he married a woman more than half his age. The marriage did not bring him the contentment he desired. He could not remember the last time he smiled and laughed. He had spent less than an hour talking with Elizabeth Peabody and had never been happier.

* * *

With his right hand, Giorgio pulled the vial of cyanide from his pocket. He reached for an appetizer with his left hand as he poured the poison into the glass of champagne Reggie had placed on the table. Amid the laughter and conversation around the table, he was certain no one noticed him. He nodded and smiled at Olivia.

"Reggie, do you hear the song playing? Our senior prom theme was *Moments to Remember*. How about a dance with an old friend?"

"Elizabeth, no one else is dancing; we will make fools of ourselves."

"Let's show these young people how it is done."

Laughing, Reggie bumped into the table as the filled champagne glasses wobbled. He stopped two or three from tipping over, disrupting their positions.

No one noticed a hand moving the tainted drink.

Looking in Olivia's direction, Georgie raised his glass in a silent toast and drank the contents as he walked away from the crowded table. *Leave it to Sophie to buy cheap champagne. This stuff tastes terrible.* As he fell to the floor, he realized he had picked up the wrong glass. It was the last thought he would ever have.

Chapter Fourteen

Sophia watches as Giorgio guzzles the champagne Travis recommended for her guests. The pained look on his face tells her he does not care for her choice. She hears a wail coming from across the room.

Tammy Sue tries to ignore the man she has begun to despise. The reassurances she received from her lawyer and new friends did not put her mind at ease. "Tammy Sue, you need another glass of champagne to calm your nerves. With any luck, Giorgio will leave soon." Olivia Talbot's shriek startled both women. They watch in surprise as Olivia throws herself onto the floor next to the unconscious Giorgio.

A stunned Reggie watches in silence as his wife sobs uncontrollably. He surmises Olivia had been having an affair with her hairdresser. Reggie did not care. He never loved Olivia and knew she had married him for his money. He had been such an unpleasant man; no decent woman would have him.

"Reggie, I have been keeping you from your wife. Go to her. She needs you."

"Olivia does not need me. I mistakenly thought a pretty, young thing would bring meaning to my life. I was wrong."

Detective Rick Madison pries Olivia off Giorgio's body. He detects the aroma of almonds which points to cyanide poisoning. After calling for help, Jessica saw Rick shake his head. The sirens could be heard in the distance. An attempt was made to revive him, but to no avail. The ambulance transported Giorgio to the morgue for examination by the coroner.

Tammy Sue's eyes fill with tears. She wished the man dead a brief time ago. Cynthia had persuaded her to get something to eat. He was across from her at the buffet table when he drank his champagne and walked away with a smug smile. It was the last time she saw her children's father alive. Tammy Sue felt Cynthia's hand on her shoulder. "It will be all right. You and the children are safe now."

Sophia's expectation that something would go wrong had come true. She never expected Giorgio to seek his revenge by dying on her new salon's floor. She looks questioningly at Travis. Did his father have anything to do with Giorgio's death? She doubted Harry Bloom would resort to poisoning a troublemaker. He might have him beaten to death or murdered by a single well-aimed bullet. Poisoning a man did not fit the mold. She has no love for Giorgio but is saddened by his death.

Jessica suspected Giorgio and Olivia Talbot were an item. Reggie Talbot is possessive of his wife. Is it possible the man knew of their affair and had his wife's lover poisoned? The thought of Mrs. Peabody spending time with the disagreeable old man troubled her. Especially if he is a murderer.

Olivia sat on a chair, staring into space until Giorgio's body was wheeled away.

Sophie approached the woman to offer her comfort. "Would you like some tea, Mrs. Talbot? It has been a terrible time for all of us."

"What do you mean a terrible time for all of us? You got what you wanted, a salon with your name on the door. You had no regard for Giorgio and how hard he worked for you ungrateful people. She pushed Sophie out of the way. And you, little innocent Tammy Sue, expecting Giorgio to give you money for kids that do not belong to him. You broke my Giorgio's heart and returned to bilk him of his money. All of you women are losers. Reggie, you are a loser too. You could not tolerate my being happy. It was you who was supposed to die, not Giorgio. How did you switch champagne glasses without being seen? If you did not switch the drinks. It was Sophie or the country bumpkin, Tammy Sue. Sophie is your boyfriend following in his old man's footsteps. Is he the newest gangster on the block proving himself by murdering Giorgio?"

"Mrs. Talbot, it is in your best interest to stop talking. I hope you will come willingly to the police station. I would like to hear more about the plan to murder your husband."

"Reggie, you cannot let him arrest me. I did nothing wrong. Call your lawyers. I am an innocent woman."

"Olivia, my dear, you are far from innocent. You have not been arrested. You have information about the plan to murder me. I am interested in what you have to say as well. Detective, may I go to the station? I would like to hear what my wife has to say?"

"Mr. Talbot, you are welcome to come to the station. We will speak with your wife alone unless you wish to call your attorney."

"That will not be necessary; let me know if you plan to arrest her."

Olivia glared at Reggie. How dare he send her off with a police detective without a lawyer present? *Why did I say Reggie was the target and not Giorgio? He will divorce me and leave me penniless. Darn you, Giorgio; you were supposed to follow the plan. I would be the grieving widow instead of being questioned by the cops.*

Travis was on his phone with his father. He had to know if Harry or his goons had anything to do with Giorgio's death. Harry had taken a liking to Sophie, and it would be like him to protect her from the likes of Giorgio.

"Son, a man was poisoned, and you suspect me? I do not mess with that stuff. It is dangerous; someone could get hurt." Harry laughed at his joke.

"That is what I thought, Dad. Sophie does not need help keeping people in line. She can manage herself without help from your friends."

"I agree, Son. I like the girl. When are you going to marry her and give me grandchildren?"

The idea of Harry Bloom being a grandfather to his children sickened Travis. He wanted a calm life for his future kids.

"Dad, Sophie and I have only known each other since New Year's Eve. It is too soon to talk about marriage."

"You had better act quickly, son. If you are not careful, someone else will snap her up. Someone like me."

"Dad, do not be disgusting."

"Hey! That was a compliment."

Travis wished he could feel affection for his father. When he made vial remarks like that, it turned him off.

* * *

Reggie Talbot drove home to his mansion on the hill. With its two pools, a tennis court, a fully equipped gym, and a movie theater, it gave him no pleasure. He remembered the house where he grew up. He wondered if it was still there. He laughed when he thought of the times, he and his friends busted the garage door window while playing ball in the backyard. His childhood and teen years were happy times. How could he have let Pamela Ellington-Ross influence his entire adulthood?

It did not surprise him that Olivia would be part of a plan to kill him. He had been a lousy husband. He could not remember why he married her in the first place. He had been involved with many beautiful women. He attended a swanky garden party in the Hamptons the week before he met her. He went to prove he fit in with the wealthy crowd. He heard his name called and recognized the voice. He turned around, expecting to see an older version of Pamela. Instead, it was like looking at a freak show. Her beautiful blonde hair was a brassy yellow. It fell to her shoulders in a style fit for someone in their twenties. She had work done on her face. He could barely see her green eyes; her cheekbones were lifted, making her eyes look like slits on her face. Her mouth was puffed to twice normal size. She wore a tank top showing off her enhanced bust. The rest of her body looked emaciated. Reggie guessed she had been starving herself. She held a martini in one hand and a cigarette in the other.

"Are you going to ignore me, Reggie? I understand you are unmarried. I hope you are not still pining away for me."

If he ever pined away for Pamela, he no longer did. He had no idea what to say to her. She reeked of cigarettes and stale booze. It was barely noon, and she was slurring her words.

The hostess approached the couple. "Come sit with your friends, Pamela. Stop pestering Mr. Talbot."

Pamela walked away with her head down. Reggie tried to hide his distaste for the woman she had become.

He had carried a vision of the beautiful girl in his mind. No one he had met measured up to his memory of Pamela. When Olivia Prince entered his life the following week, he saw a resemblance to the young Pamela and asked her to marry him. He knew she loved his money, not him. He did not care.

* * *

At the police station, Olivia denied her earlier statement claiming there was no truth to her comments. It devastated her that a man was killed before her eyes. She barely knew Giorgio. He was not her lover.

"Why not question Sophie Clark? She hated Giorgio and never made a secret of it. That little hick who claims to be Giorgio's wife had more reason to kill him than anyone. You should be questioning my husband. If Reggie thought I had an affair with Giorgio, he would kill him. I was not, but Reggie is a jealous man."

Rick had no reason to detain her. Emotion could have led her to make false statements. He believed she told the truth at the salon but needed more information about where the poison came from. It had to be in a container. Where is that container? His men had done a thorough search and turned up nothing.

"Olivia, an officer will drive you home. We will contact you if we have any further questions."

Olivia did not want to go home to face Reggie. What if he intended to divorce her and leave her impoverished? Giorgio, why did you have to go and die on me? She had nowhere else to go. She had no key to Giorgio's apartment. She had to go home and face the music.

Chapter Fifteen

Olivia dared not call for the Talbot limousine to take her home from the police station. Having an emotional breakdown over Giorgio surely caused Reggie embarrassment. If only she had held herself together. There was time for tears after the cops had arrested the person responsible for Giorgio's death.

When she discovered he had swallowed the poisoned champagne intended for Reggie, she erupted in shock. How did it happen? No one knew of their plans; she had not told a soul.

As the cab driver pulled onto the circular driveway, she saw Reggie standing at the door holding a suitcase.

He is throwing me out. He will not let me go into the mansion. Where will I go?

Olivia is surprised to see her husband pull cash from his pocket and hand it to the driver. After depositing his suitcase into his car, he turned to her, saying they needed to talk. "Come inside, Olivia. I will not keep you long."

Following him inside, Olivia held her head high. She would beg his forgiveness for the way she carried on about Giorgio. He must be convinced her reaction was caused by seeing someone die. She would claim she barely knew Giorgio.

"Do not lie, Olivia. You and your friend planned to kill me off and live happily ever after on my money. The man was a user. You are better off without him. You are better off without me as well. We married for all the wrong reasons. I wanted someone who would make me feel young again. You wanted someone who would provide you with luxury. Marrying you did not make me young and marrying me did not make you happy."

"I will be happy, Reggie, and I will be a good wife to you. I promise."

"You are willing to live in a loveless marriage for money. I am not. It has taken me years to realize the wealth I strived for only made me a cantankerous old fool. In a few minutes, I will be leaving the mansion. You may continue to live here for as long as you wish. I am sure you will agree to a divorce. I hope you find someone who will love you and make you happy."

Olivia stared at him in disbelief. "It is that old lady to whom you were talking. You two were chummy. Did she tell you to dump me?"

"That old lady is a dear friend from my youth. After all these years, she brought me to my senses. If you do not agree to a divorce, my offer is withdrawn. You have twenty-four hours to make up your mind."

Reggie drove his car away from the mansion and Olivia. He felt free for the first time in many years.

Olivia poured herself a stiff drink. She glanced in the mirror. *I am still in my prime. With Reggie's money, men will flock to me. The old guy must have had a nervous breakdown. Who cares; he is giving me his money, and I cannot wait to spend it.*

* * *

A container with the remnants of cyanide could not be found at the scene. Rick believed Giorgio and Olivia were involved in a scheme that went wrong. Due to the lack of evidence and Olivia's insistence she barely knew the man, the case against her was weak.

The champagne glasses were swapped either accidentally or deliberately. Reggie Talbot admitted to bumping into the table and saving the filled glasses from tipping over. He wondered if he had inadvertently switched glasses. Talbot insisted he had no clue there was poison in any of the drinks.

Rick could not shake the feeling there was more to the mystery than an accidental mix-up with the drinks. He met Tammy Sue Henshaw for the first time today. She presented herself as a shy country girl who did what needed to be done to keep her children from poverty. It is possible she saw Giorgio pour the liquid into Reggie's glass and switched drinks. It made little sense. Tammy Sue and Cynthia Brainard were together continuously during the party. Cynthia would have stopped Tammy Sue from touching Giorgio's glass.

There was no love lost between Sophie and Giorgio. Sophie was finally free of the man and his hold over her. There was no reason to kill him now.

Did Reggie Talbot know of his wife's infidelity with Giorgio? Poisoning his wife's lover in a room full of people would be a stupid move. Reggie Talbot is not a stupid man. If he wanted Giorgio dead, there were many ways to accomplish his goal without getting his hands dirty.

The three possible suspects were called to the station. Tammy Sue was the first to arrive with Cynthia Brainard by her side.

"Detective Madison, is my client a suspect in the murder of the man she knows as Hank Henshaw? I can assure you; Mrs. Henshaw never left my side during the salon open house."

Tammy Sue was visibly shaken as she sat with her hands folded in her lap.

"With your permission, I would like to ask Mrs. Henshaw questions related to the death of her husband."

Cynthia turns to her client, "Tammy Sue, it is Detective Madison's job to question those who might have information about Hank's death. Answer his questions truthfully; you have nothing to hide."

Rick listens as Tammy Sue talks about her children. It is clear she had their best interest at heart when attempting to force her husband to help her financially. Rick has no sympathy for a man who would abandon his wife and children. He does not think Tammy Sue caused her husband's death.

* * *

Sophie walks into Rick's office, holding Travis's hand.

"Detective, I was with Sophie when she approached the buffet table. I can assure you; she was nowhere near Giorgio when he drank the laced drink."

"Sophie, I want to ask you about the cyanide. Was the poison in your shop? Is it possible the former tenant left it?"

"No, I do not have cyanide in my shop or in my home. Agnes Weatherby sold fabric in the space for thirty years. She always had a cat to take care of any rodents that found their way into the basement. She had no reason to keep poison in the building."

"Did you see Giorgio pick up a glass of champagne?"

"I did not notice. Mr. Talbot was talking to Mrs. Peabody when he bumped into the table, causing the filled glasses to wobble. He caught them before they tipped over. The next thing I knew, Giorgio had collapsed."

"You did not see Mr. Talbot drop anything into the glasses or switch them so Giorgio would pick up the glass meant for him?"

"Unless he is a magician, he could not have slipped cyanide or anything into the glass. He straightened them without changing their position. The man had been talking to Elizabeth Peabody for a long time. They were having an enjoyable time. Mr. Talbot smiled; he even laughed a few times. I have heard the man is the town grouch."

"It is true," offered Travis, "Reggie Talbot is known for his sour disposition. I had never seen him smile before the party. Mrs. Peabody accomplished something his beautiful wife could not."

"How well do you know Olivia Talbot, Travis?"

"Not well at all. She and my mother participate in some charitable events together. I have heard my mother complain about Olivia being a gold digger. It takes one to know one."

Sophie snickered, "She must think the same thing about me."

"You are free to go. I am sorry this happened in your new salon, Sophie."

"Thanks Detective; It looks like Giorgio got the last laugh."

* * *

Reggie Talbot sat in the chair opposite Rick.

"I was not the one who poisoned Giorgio. If I wanted the man dead, I would have arranged for it to happen. The way he and my wife looked at each other, I knew there was something going on. You might not believe me when I say I did not care. Olivia and I made a mistake when we married fifteen years ago. We never loved each other."

"Why were you at the open house? What was your interest in a beauty salon?"

"I had no interest in it. Harry Bloom lent me money when I opened my real-estate business. It was another mistake on my part. I've long since paid him back. One never gets out from under Harry Bloom's thumb. He asked me to attend in his place, and I obliged. He did not want to scare off the girl's customers by showing up himself."

"What a guy!" Rick said under his breath. "I understand you arranged the filled glasses after you bumped into the table."

The man's eyes took on a new light, and he smiled. "Elizabeth Peabody is an old classmate of mine. I had not seen her in many years. She suggested we dance to a tune playing in the background. I tried to protest, saying we would look foolish being the only dancers. She pulled my arm, and I knocked the table. If I had known Giorgio was about to poison me, I would have had him arrested, not killed him."

Rick bids the older gentleman good night. He had three suspects who were close to the champagne glasses. He did not believe any had been responsible for Giorgio's death. Olivia Talbot lied to him about being Giorgio's lover with knowledge of his plans to kill her husband. He assumed she changed her story to escape her husband's wrath. Rick hoped Jessica was not asleep. He wanted to get her opinion about what might have happened.

Chapter Sixteen

The woman stared out the window, watching the stars blink in the sky. *I have gotten away with murder.* She thought to herself, with a sense of relief.

* * *

Jessica waited for Rick's familiar knock on her apartment door. From the exasperated look on his face, she knew he was perplexed by Giorgio's murder.

"This should be an open and shut case. Giorgio poisoned another man's drink and somehow drank it himself. What caused him to confuse the tainted champagne with his glass? It makes no sense. He did not walk away from the table after pouring the cyanide into Reggie Talbot's glass. What made him drink the champagne? If he had waited across the room for Reggie to drink his drink, he would have avoided detection. Olivia would perform her grieving widow act, and no one would know Giorgio was the culprit."

"Rick, Giorgio's ego would not let him believe his plan would go awry. His act fooled many people, but mostly himself. He thought he was infallible."

"I need your instinct. You have a knack for solving mysteries. Who do you think switched the glasses?" Rick explained why he had eliminated the obvious suspects.

"Olivia changed her initial story about her affair with Giorgio. When questioned at the police station, she denied a relationship claiming she was shocked by the man dying before her eyes. Either story did not prove her guilty in Giorgio's death. She could be implicated as an accomplice in her husband's attempted murder.

"Unless Tammy Sue Henshaw is a fraud, she is too timid to commit murder, Cynthia was close to her during the party. Tammy Sue would have to be an expert at sleight of hand to switch the glasses without being noticed. She had no way of knowing her husband planned to murder Reggie Talbot.

"Sophie might have been irked that Giorgio crashed her open house, but it would not be enough to provoke her into causing his death. She did not know he planned to create a scene in her new salon by killing his lover's husband.

"Reggie Talbot might have known of his wife's affair. As he said, if he wanted Giorgio dead, he would have hired someone to carry out the deed without implicating him."

Jessica thought for a moment. "You have questioned the obvious suspects. It is not feasible that any of them committed the murder. We are missing a piece of the puzzle. Assuming no one knew of Giorgio's plans except Olivia, the glass mix-up could have been an accident. Giorgio might have boasted about his plans to someone, but that is doubtful. Short of questioning everyone who attended the party, we should look for motives."

"I love the look on your face when you are in your sleuthing mode."

Rick took her in his arms. "Shall we sleep on it and start fresh in the morning? The puzzle pieces might fit better after a good night's sleep."

"I am not sleepy, are you?" Jessica took his hand, leading him into the bedroom. The subject of Giorgio's murder was far from Rick's mind.

* * *

Reggie checked into the Brentwood Hotel. He would find a place to live in the morning. He felt a burden had been lifted from his shoulders. His marriage to Olivia had been a mistake from the beginning. She is still a beautiful woman. She and the hairdresser planned to kill him and live happily ever after on his money. He chuckled thinking of the expression on her face when he told her the mansion was hers if she agreed to a divorce. She refused to admit she had been unfaithful. He is happy to be alive and will not waste another day striving for wealth and power.

Reggie knew he would be unable to sleep, He drove to the old neighborhood where he had not been in years. The houses all looked the same. He saw a swing hanging from a branch of a large tree in front of his old house. He remembered the day his father planted it. He had watered it in the summer and clearing the snow from it in the winter. *If only pop could see it now. His tender loving care resulted in this fabulous tree.*

He remembered the house where Elizabeth lived. She had mentioned moving back home to help her mother and staying on long after her parents' passed. He drove to her house. The lights glowed in the window. After glancing at his watch, he wondered if ten o'clock was too late for a social call. He took a chance she would not call the police when he rang her doorbell.

"Who is it?" A soft voice called from behind the closed door.

"Elizabeth, it is Reggie. I know it is late, but I hoped you would be awake."

The door flew open. "Reggie, I am so happy to see you. I heard you were being questioned about Giorgio's death. Are you okay?"

"I am better than okay. I have you to thank for reminding me what is important in life. I have left Olivia and the mansion. She is welcome to it after she agrees to a divorce. I have been recalling my youth. I let a silly girl influence me several years ago. I finally came to my senses. Money means nothing if it is the only goal in life. I will turn over my business to my capable staff and find a small apartment in this neighborhood. Will you agree to have dinner with me occasionally?"

"Why would you rent an apartment when this house has a private residence where you can stay? It has a kitchen and bath. You would have complete privacy. Though I will take you up on your dinner invitation."

"That sounds perfect. I had no idea you had extra space for a tenant."

"My folks built it when my grandparents were alive. They wanted them close but not underfoot. I lived there before and after I married Hector Peabody. Hector never made much money, but he was a happy man."

"How could he not be happy married to you, Elizabeth?"

"You do not have to butter me up, Reggie. You already have the apartment."

The two settled on the sofa, talking, and continuing to catch up on each other's lives. The grandfather clock in the hallway struck midnight.

"I have overstayed my welcome, Elizabeth. The time has flown. I will be by tomorrow. Not too early since I have kept you up so late tonight."

"I have enjoyed our talk. It will be good to have someone in this old house. I have thought of selling it; I am glad I never did."

Reggie gave Elizabeth a peck on the cheek. His step was light as he made his way to his car.

Chapter Seventeen

It was ten minutes after nine when Reggie's phone rang. At this hour, he is usually awake and sitting at his desk in his office.

"Reggie, it is Melbourne Gleason. I just had a call from Oscar Maynard. He is representing Olivia in her request for divorce. The woman is living in your home. I will call the police and have her removed."

"Melbourne do not do that. Olivia is the new owner of the Talbot mansion. Or she will be when you arrange for the title to be transferred to her. I want nothing to do with the place. I also want you to set up a continuing trust for her. Double the size of her allowance."

"Has the woman drugged you? You cannot turn everything over to her. She and her lover planned to kill you."

"You heard about that. The plan went awry, and Olivia's boyfriend ended up dead. I had an epiphany yesterday. All these years. I have been seeking my fortune. I exceeded my goals and discovered I was nothing but an irritable old man. I want you to sell my portion of the business to my staff. Make it a reasonable price they can afford. I am retired as of now."

After arguing with his client for thirty minutes, Melbourne acknowledged the man had not lost his mind. He is serious about living a simple life. *The sly old fox has met a woman who is not after his money. Good for him.*

* * *

Olivia woke with a throbbing head. She reaches for her hand mirror to examine her face for flaws after a night of drinking. She chastises herself for overindulging as her skin has taken on a sallow hue. *I cannot believe I am the owner of the mansion. When Reggie heard my ideas for rearranging the space, he frowned. Everything is so formal and dismal. I will transform it into a showplace. The color purple will be dominant throughout in memory of poor Giorgio. I wonder who killed him? It works out better this way. I will not have to share my money with anyone.*

* * *

Tammy Sue packs her suitcase, leaving the dress she borrowed from Cynthia for the Salon Opening on a hanger.

Cynthia arrives at the hotel room. She insists Tammy Sue keep the dress. The grateful young woman hugs her new friend and lawyer. "I have never owned anything as pretty as this dress. Are you sure the police will let me go home to my children? I witnessed Hank's death." She said with a shiver,

"You are not a suspect. Rick Madison gave the okay for you to leave Brentwood. He will call you back if he needs more information. You and the children will benefit from his lucrative business. I will miss you, my friend. Hug the children for me; I hope to meet them in person one day soon."

Tammy Sue's eyes fill with tears as the bus pulls away from the station. *Brentwood would be a good place for children to grow up.*

* * *

Sophie grieved for the loss of life. She had reason to dislike Giorgio but never wished him dead. Thanks to her friends, the salon's opening was successful until Giorgio collapsed. The incident haunted Sophie's dreams last night. Did Giorgio hate her enough to ruin her grand opening by committing murder? Sophie recalled watching Giorgio fawn over Olivia Talbot at the New Year's Eve party. Was it a simple flirtation or the start of a plan to kill Reggie Talbot?

Worried about Sophie, Travis stopped to see her on his way to the office.

"When did the police say you could open the shop?"

"It will be another week. The cyanide container is still missing. My day will be quite different than I had anticipated. I have arranged for Giorgio's stylists to fit everyone in at his place. I cannot make my customers wait another week or more to have their hair done."

Travis's heart broke for Sophie. Her opening would be delayed after putting so much work into her new place. Most anyone else would complain about the unfairness, not Sophie. She is more concerned about a dead man who does not deserve her sympathy after planning to ruin her party.

* * *

Jessica brushes her hair back off her face. She is overdue for a haircut but wanted her next one to be at Sophie's Salon. Sophie called her earlier, saying she had arranged for Mindy to do her hair that morning.

"Sophie, I have waited this long; another week will not kill me. Besides, Rick thinks the new me is sexy."

"You misheard him; he meant your new look is shaggy. I insist you see Mindy this morning. She knows how you like to wear your hair."

Jessica finally agreed. It would allow her to speak to the stylists who attended the open house. She hoped someone had information to help solve the mystery.

* * *

As his wealth increased, he wore clothes that were too formal for the life he planned to live. Using the hotel's dry-cleaning bag, he filled it with the clothing he had brought with them. On his way to Elizabeth's house, he would stop at the closest men's shop. On second thought, he would stop in the city's mall for his purchases. Trying to look like a normal retiree was his goal. *I will buy a pair of tennis shoes.* He chuckled to himself.

He refrained from calling the bellman to carry his belongings to his car. He would enjoy doing things for himself again. As he checked out, he handed the desk clerk the bag filled with clothes.

"Young man will you deliver these to the local shelter or thrift store? Here is something for your trouble." Reggie handed the clerk a hundred-dollar bill.

Reggie realized he had no idea what to buy at the department store. He picked up two shirts and pants. He hoped Elizabeth would come with him and help him decide what was appropriate for a man of leisure.

Reggie arrived at Elizabeth's front door, suitcase in hand. "I hope you haven't changed your mind."

"I have been busy all morning freshening your rooms. I hope you will be comfortable here. The appliances are older, but they do work."

"The last time I used an oven was in college, and it was a microwave. I will order out for my dinner."

"Nonsense, I would love to cook for you. You can eat with me, or I will leave the meal at your doorstep if you prefer to be alone."

"I would prefer to be with you. We cannot have you cooking every evening. I will take you to dinner on the days you work."

Chapter Eighteen

Jessica opened the door to Salon di Giorgio's. A variety of purple shades caused her to blink. Thee understated elegance of Sophie's Salon made Giorgio's place seem garish in comparison. Soft music played in the background emphasizing the somberness of the staff and customers.

Mindy greeted Jessica in a quiet voice. "This place is full of gloom and doom over Giorgio's death."

"People are still in shock over seeing a man die before their eyes. It is a natural reaction."

"I suppose so. I was not there when Giorgio died." Mindy exclaimed. "I did not feel well and left early."

Jessica did not respond to Mindy's comment. Everyone behaves differently in a situation like this. If she had not witnessed his collapse, she might not have felt the impact as those who did.

Mindy said little as she washed Jessica's hair. After returning to the styling chair, Jessica thought the girl seemed nervous. She assured her she was not worried about the girl trimming her hair. "As you can see, I am not overly concerned with my hairstyle. As long as my bangs are not covering my eyes, I am happy."

Though she tried to hide it, Mindy's hands trembled.

"Mindy, what is wrong? Are you feeling ill? We can do this another day if you need to go home."

"I am fine. I felt a chill from the air conditioner. Tell me, Jessica, does Detective Madison have a suspect in Giorgio's murder?"

"It might have been an accident. Giorgio planned to poison Reggie Talbot's drink, but the glasses were switched, and Giorgio drank the tainted champagne by mistake. Mindy, do you know something about the incident? If you do, you must tell Detective Madison."

"I do not know anything. I left the party before Giorgio drank that stupid drink."

Jessica sensed the girl was hiding something. If she pushed, Mindy would clam up. Instead, she commented on the work Sophie put into her new salon and how it paid off. "I remember seeing you helping her decorate her new place. I love the color scheme; it is relaxing and not overwhelming."

"I did not do much. Sophie knew what she wanted; I simply tagged along on her shopping trips. Giorgio found out I was helping her and threatened that he would report me to the licensing board, and I would lose my license."

"Helping a friend would not be an offense. He was trying to get your goat. I wish you had checked with Meredith Donovan. Giorgio's threat might have been enough to allow you to break your contract with him."

"Mindy, you did a terrific job with my hair. It is just the way I like it."

She left the salon wondering if Mindy had the missing puzzle piece. The girl was holding back. Jessica wondered why.

* * *

Elizabeth Peabody drove to the Steven Gray Law office in her little yellow Volkswagen as she had for years.

"Mr. Gray, may I speak with you?"

"Come in, Elizabeth; how may I help you?" Steve said softly. He has always been fond of her.

"I have enjoyed working at the firm for these many years. My time here has been my lifesaver. The young lawyers and all the staff have been like the children I never had. I have become reacquainted with a high-school friend. He has talked about traveling to places I have only dreamt about. Our relationship is strictly platonic. Though it breaks my heart, I cannot be in two places at one time. I am giving my notice." A tear formed in her eye.

"Elizabeth, I speak for the firm when I say we hate to lose you. You have been like a mother hen to all of us. It is wonderful you have renewed an old friendship and will be traveling. It is with regret I accept your resignation. I know Karen and the girls will insist on giving you a fabulous retirement party."

"That would be marvelous. May I invite my new tenant?"

"Of course, Mr. Talbot will be welcome to join us."

"How did you know my friend is Reggie Talbot?"

"I saw him flirting with you the night of Sophie's open house."

"Reggie did no such thing." Elizabeth's eyes told a different story.

* * *

Jessica stopped by Sophie's apartment to ask about Mindy.

"Your hair looks great. I am glad Mindy did a good job for you. How is she feeling? I know she left the open house early. She said she was not feeling well. She seemed all right when I spoke with her yesterday."

"She did not appear ill; she acted nervously. Her hand began to tremble when she held the scissors to my head."

"Really! I cannot believe she was intimidated by you. She considers you a friend, as I do."

"I feel the same way. It is why this is so awkward. Mindy left before Giorgio collapsed. She believed he had been murdered. I made it clear that his death could have been an accident. She continued to dwell on the incident. Did she tell you he threatened to have her license revoked because she helped you in the new salon?"

"Mindy is naïve and gullible, but why would she believe such a thing? Are you saying she switched those drinks and killed Giorgio?"

"No, I do not think she is capable of murder. She knows more than she is telling."

"I will talk to her. If she knows something, I will get it out of her."

The unlocked door opened. Mindy appeared with tears filling her eyes.

"I will tell you everything, Jessica. You can call Detective Madison. I am ready to confess to killing Giorgio."

Jessica implored the girl not to say anything until a lawyer could be present. She suggested calling Travis Bloom as he has proven to be a competent defense attorney.

* * *

"Travis has agreed to represent you; he will meet us at the police station where Detective Madison is waiting."

* * *

At the station, Travis talked to Mindy. She told him her story. He saw no reason for her not to talk to Rick Madison. Rick is a fair man who will listen to the facts.

Sophie handed Rick the vial of poison. A small amount of liquid was at the bottom.

"Why do you have this, Mindy?"

"I took it after I had moved the glasses so Giorgio could not hurt anyone. He left it on the table next to the champagne glasses. He wanted Sophie blamed for the death of Mr. Talbot."

"How did you know Mr. Talbot was his target?"

"I should start from the beginning. I had no appointments after lunch on the night of the open house. I had planned to help Sophie with any last-minute details.

"I was ready to walk out the door when Giorgio called me into his office. He discovered I had helped Sophie decorate her new shop. He threatened me that he could have my license taken away. I believed he would do it. I was upset and walked out, leaving my keys in the chair. I walked the few blocks to my apartment before I realized I had left my door key behind. About thirty minutes had passed when I decided I had to return to his office to collect my keys.

"The other stylists had gone. They also planned to attend the open house and did not schedule appointments for the afternoon. The salon door was unlocked. I walked in, thinking Giorgio would be alone. I heard voices coming from the office. I was going to knock on the door, grab my keys and leave quickly. That is when I overheard their conversation.

"He called the woman Olivia. I knew she was Olivia Talbot. The woman came into the shop occasionally to have her hair done. We all speculated that she and Giorgio were involved. I was going to turn around and leave, but I needed my keys. I backed into an alcove where I heard their conversation. He said he would put cyanide in the old man's drink. He would die instantly, and it will look like Sophie's carelessness caused his death. Giorgio laughed as though killing a man was a joke. Olivia laughed along with him. They talked about the money she would get, and they would go off to some island and live in luxury. Olivia said she could not wait to play the grieving widow and laughed again. They did not see me as they left arm in arm.

"I should have called the police, but Giorgio would deny what he said. He would tell them I was angry because he planned to report me to the licensing board. I hoped I could talk him out of his plan at the party.

"Later, I saw Mrs. Peabody talking to Reggie Talbot. I could see the happiness in her eyes and his. I cut Mrs. Peabody's hair sometimes. She is kind to me. I could not let Giorgio kill the man who put a smile on her face. I saw Giorgio fill the glass with poison. When he turned away, I moved that glass away from Mr. Talbot, thinking no one would drink it. I took the vial from the table and put it in my purse. I did not lie when I said I did not feel well. The whole scene made me sick. I went home, taking the poison with me. Giorgio was alive when I left the salon.

"It haunts me that I almost got away with murder. I am ready to face the consequences now."

"Mindy, you did not commit murder. You saved Reggie Talbot's life. If you had not moved those glasses, he would be dead now. Giorgio died by his own hand, though it was not part of his plan."

Chapter Nineteen

Detective Madison arrived at the Talbot mansion to question Olivia Talbot further.

The woman denied knowledge of a plan to murder her husband. Mindy had not seen Olivia and could not identify Giorgio's accomplice. The district attorney agreed that the case against Olivia Talbot was weak. Giorgio's death was ruled an accident.

Mindy was praised for saving Reggie Talbot's life. Grateful for her quick thinking, Mrs. Peabody unofficially adopted Mindy as a granddaughter.

Reggie waited impatiently for his divorce from Olivia to be finalized. He wanted to be a free man before asking Elizabeth to marry him. If he moved to the main house, the apartment would be available for Mindy. The girl visited often, but Reggie knew it would make Elizabeth happy to have her living in the same house. Though retired, he still had influence in town and was granted a divorce in a matter of weeks. Elizabeth accepted Reggie's proposal.

They were married in an intimate ceremony with Mindy and Steven Gray as witnesses. Mindy moved into the apartment vacated by Reggie the following week.

Giorgio's estate was settled. He was not a wealthy man but had accumulated enough money to ensure Tammy Sue and her children a secure future. The Casa di Giorgio building was sold to a restaurant chain. The salon furnishings and equipment were auctioned, with the profit going to his widow. Tammy Sue purchased a home in Brentwood for her parents and the children.

* * * *

The country club's ballroom was the venue for Elizabeth's retirement party.

Reggie Talbot sat proudly next to his wife at the head table. He marveled at the number of friends and acquaintances in attendance. Steven Gray made a speech that brought tears to his eyes. He felt remorse that he had wasted his life on things that did not matter. Elizabeth squeezed his hand as she whispered, "The best is yet to come."

Epilogue

Business is thriving at Sophie's Salon. Soon after the police closed their inquiry into Giorgio's death, her former coworkers joined her team. Sophie refused to require signed contracts from her stylists. In the event that anyone wanted to join another shop or venture out on their own, she would not stand in their way.

No one took her up on her offer. Sophie is a kind and generous owner. The atmosphere in the salon is in direct contrast to the rigidity of the former Casa di Giorgio.

* * *

Mindy's confidence has been restored since living in the Talbot household. She has a family in Elizabeth and Reggie. Though officially retired, Reggie encourages his former staff to call with questions about the company he had controlled for years. He is impressed with a young man in the accounting department, not only for his work ethic but for his sparkling personality. Tanner Colby accepts a dinner invitation to the Talbot home. When Mindy Lawrence appears as they are having cocktails, she apologizes for interrupting their visit.

"Nonsense, come sit next to Tanner." Reggie introduces the two. By the end of the evening, it is clear that Reggie has a knack for matchmaking.

* * *

Tammy Sue accepts a job in the elementary school where Timothy and Melissa are enrolled. The children ask questions about their father. When they were young, Tammy Sue told them their father had gone away. After questioning when he would come back, Tammy Sue revealed he had died. Some day she would tell them about Giorgio and how he died. She hoped they would not resent her for lying all these years. Few people in Brentwood knew Giorgio was the father of Tammy Sue's children. Those who do, never talk about it.

* * *

Travis Bloom receives a call from Brentwood Hospital late in the evening. He and Sophie are watching an old movie on television. Suddenly his face loses its color.

"Travis, what is it?"

"My father had a heart attack; he died on the way to the hospital."

Not knowing what to say, Sophie wraps her arms around him.

"Do I feel sadness or relief? I disliked his line of work, but he was my father. He was not all bad."

"Think of the good in him. He cared for you and protected you from harm."

"Sophie, I love you. I have wanted to ask you to be my wife for months. With my criminal father in the picture, I had no right to marry you and bring a gangster's grandchildren into the world. Is it too soon for me to ask you to marry me now that he is gone."

"I would like nothing better than to marry you. Shall we talk about it when your shock wears off?"

"We can wait, but I will not change my mind."

* * *

Harry Bloom's passing was in all the area newspapers. The scandal-prone tabloids reported he had been in his mistress's bed at the time of his death. Sylvia discounted that fact and acted as the grieving widow until Harry's coffin was lowered into his grave.

"Though it is better for the environment, my mother insisted he not be cremated. Throwing herself on a casket is a much better photo op than holding an urn in her arms. I cannot believe you still want to marry the son of Harry and Sylvia Bloom. My gene pool is lacking in decency."

"Travis Bloom, you lack nothing. You have broken the cycle. I cannot wait to have your babies."

* * *

After a barbeque in Steve and Karen Gray's backyard, Steve turns to Rick and Jessica.

"What are you two waiting for? Jessica, I have tried never to interfere in your life, but I cannot understand why you two are not married. If you wait much longer, your mother and I will be too old to enjoy our grandchildren."

"Your dad has a good question, Jessie; why haven't you married me?"

"I do not remember you asking me, Ricky Madison."

"I am asking you now. Will you marry me?"

"I thought you would never ask. The answer is yes."

Rick and Jessica were married on a beautiful spring day in Chelsea Gardens. The childhood sweethearts would go on to have three children. The authors continue writing mystery stories and hope the mysteries exist only in their imaginations, not in Brentwood.

Murder in Sophie's Salon is the last of the Jessica Gray series.

Other Jessica Gray Cozy Mysteries

Murder in Brentwood
Murder in Chelsea Gardens
Murder at Cromwell, Inc.

www.ingramcontent.com/pod-product-compliance
Lightning Source LLC
LaVergne TN
LVHW020010170826
845677LV00022B/2336
9798836774059